Lunch with Little Miss Muffet

Characters

Narrator

Little Miss Muffet

Ant

Curds and Whey

Spider

Setting

A clearing in the woods

Picture Words

frightened

lunch

Sight Words

am	away	do	go
I	like	little	what

milk

tuffet

Enrichment Words

along	beside
friend	low

Narrator: Little Miss Muffet, please sit on this tuffet.

 Little Miss Muffet: This what?

 Narrator: Tuffet. A tuffet is a low seat.

 Muffet: I like a low seat. I am little!

Ant: I am little.

 Narrator: Please sit down. Time for lunch.

 Ant: Good!

 Muffet: What is for lunch?

 Curds and Whey: Us. Curds and whey.

 Muffet: What and what?

 Curds and Whey: Curds and whey. We are made from milk.

 Muffet: Oh. I like milk.

 Narrator: Look what is coming along—a spider.

 Muffet: Spider? Where?

 Ant: Look!

 Spider: Here I am!

 Muffet: Spider!

Narrator: And he just sat down beside you.

 Spider: Hi!

 Muffet: Eww!

 Curds and Whey: Oh!
He is cute.

Muffet: Go away, Spider. Go away.

 Spider: I am nice.

 Muffet: I do not like spiders.

 Ant: I do not like spiders.

Curds and Whey: He wants to be your friend.

 Ant: Bye!

11

 Muffet: Good-bye!

 Narrator: Wait! Oh well. You frightened Miss Muffet away, Spider.

 Spider: I get that a lot . . .

The End